M Is For Mistletoe

A Christmas Alphabet Book

Dedicated to the warm memories of Christmases celebrated with DaddyBo, Laurie, Stacy, Steven, and–of course–Blue dog. –T.L.S.

Library of Congress Cataloging-in-Publication Data is available.

ISBN: 0-8431-0511-9   A B C D E F G H I J

M Is For Mistletoe

A Christmas Alphabet Book

By Tanya Lee Stone ❄ Illustrated by Claudine Gévry

PSS!
PRICE STERN SLOAN

A is for angels

We make in the snow
Christmas is here
And December winds blow!

B is for boxes

That reach to the sky
Armfuls of packages
Towering high!

C is for carolers

Singing a song
Passing out candy canes
Strolling along!

Holiday
Gift Drive

D is for decorate

Stockings and bows
Lights in the garlands
The whole house just glows!

E is for evergreen

Fresh-smelling pine
Shimmering Christmas tree
See the star shine!

F is for "Feliz Navidad!"
When friends come and say
"Merry Christmas," in Spanish,
On this special day!

G is for gingerbread
House that we'll eat.
Covered with gumdrops,
And candies so sweet!

H is for Ho-Ho-Ho!

Santa is near
The jolliest sound
Ringing out loud and clear!

I is for icicles

Scattering light
Twinkling and sparkling
A beautiful sight!

J is for jingle bells

Jangling bright
Our sleigh glides along
On a crisp, starry night!

K is for kitchen

Sweet smells fill the air
Hot chocolate and cookies
Warm treats we all share!

L is for letter

"Dear Santa," I write,
"I'll try to stay up
So I see you tonight!"

M is for mistletoe

Mommy, and me!
Daddy joins in
It's a kiss for all three!

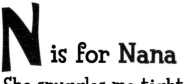

N is for Nana
She snuggles me tight
We sit by the fire
And sing "Silent Night."

O is for ornaments
That hang on our tree
Each one is different
All special to me!

P is for peace

I draw cards with a dove
To show that this season
Is filled with our love!

Q is for **quiet**
Snow gently drifts down
A cozy white blanket
That covers our town.

R is for **reindeer**
They pull Santa's sleigh
I wish I could see them—
Just once fly away!

S is for stockings

All hung in a row
Stuffed full of treasures
From tip-top to toe!

T is for toys

But they're not the best part
Our true Christmas spirit
Comes straight from the heart!

U is for unicycle

So shiny and new
A wonderful gift
From my great Uncle Stu!

V is for visitors
Who drop by all day
Neighbors and friends
Coming over to play!

W is for wise men

Dressed up for our play
They follow a bright star
That lights up their way!

Xxxx's for Kisses

That leave a red trace
From aunts and my Nana—
All over my face!

Y is for yuletide

The season of cheer
Warmth and goodwill
That will last us all year!

Z is for zipped up
All ready to rest
I hope that your Christmas
Is simply the best!